NFL'S GREATEST PLAYERS

SUPER BOWL MVPs

By Kevin Frederickson

Kaleidoscope
Minneapolis, MN

Your Front Row Seat to the Games

This edition first published in 2020 by Kaleidoscope Publishing, Inc.

For information regarding permission, write to
Kaleidoscope Publishing, Inc.
6012 Blue Circle Drive
Minnetonka, MN 55343

Library of Congress Control Number
2019939224

ISBN
978-1-64519-075-2 (library bound)
978-1-64494-174-4 (paperback)
978-1-64519-176-6 (ebook)

Printed in the United States of America.

TABLE OF CONTENTS

CHAPTER 1

Run for Glory

Terrell Davis runs onto the field. Fans cheer for the star running back. Davis and the Denver Broncos are ready. They are playing the Green Bay Packers in Super Bowl XXXII.

Quarterback John Elway snaps the ball. He hands off to Davis. Davis takes off down the field. A Packers defender tries to tackle him. But Davis spins away. Another Packers defender finally brings him down. A few plays later, Davis gets the **handoff** again. He dives one yard into the **end zone**. Touchdown!

BACK-TO-BACK CHAMPS

One Super Bowl win was not enough for the Broncos. Davis and Elway were back the next year. This time Elway was the Most Valuable Player (MVP). The Broncos faced the Atlanta Falcons. Elway hit receiver Rod Smith for an 80-yard touchdown. Elway passed for 336 yards in the game. He also ran for a touchdown. Denver won 34–19.

Terrell Davis carries the ball in Super Bowl XXXII.

Davis performs the "Mile High Salute" celebration after scoring in the third quarter.

Davis is on a roll. He runs four more times on Denver's next **drive**. The Broncos score again. Now they lead 14–7. But Davis is not well. Coaches and doctors look him over. He looks **frustrated**. A painful headache makes it hard for him to see. Davis puts a towel over his face. He doesn't want anyone to see him in pain.

Davis decides to keep playing. He returns after halftime. He even scores another touchdown. But the Packers answer. The game is tied 24–24 in the fourth quarter.

FUN FACT

Sports journalists and fans get a vote on who wins Super Bowl MVP.

Davis holds up the Super Bowl trophy following the Broncos' win.

Time is running out. But Denver keeps going back to Davis. The Broncos are at Green Bay's 18-yard line. Elway hands off to Davis again. He runs all the way to the 1-yard line. Then it is Davis's time once more. The Broncos line creates a hole. Davis runs right in. Touchdown!

That was all Denver needed. The Broncos won 31–24. Davis led the team with three touchdowns. He was named Super Bowl MVP. Davis led the Broncos all year. And he was there when they needed him most.

CHAPTER 2

Making a Difference

Drew Brees drops back to pass. He and the New Orleans Saints are two yards from the end zone. They trail the Indianapolis Colts by one point. Fewer than six minutes remain in Super Bowl XLIV. It is after the 2009 season. Brees knows he needs to make a big play.

He finds tight end Jeremy Shockey. A defender is right on him. But it's too late. Shockey falls into the end zone. Touchdown! The Saints go on to win 31–17. Brees is named Super Bowl MVP.

FUN FACT

Brees threw for 288 yards in Super Bowl XLIV.

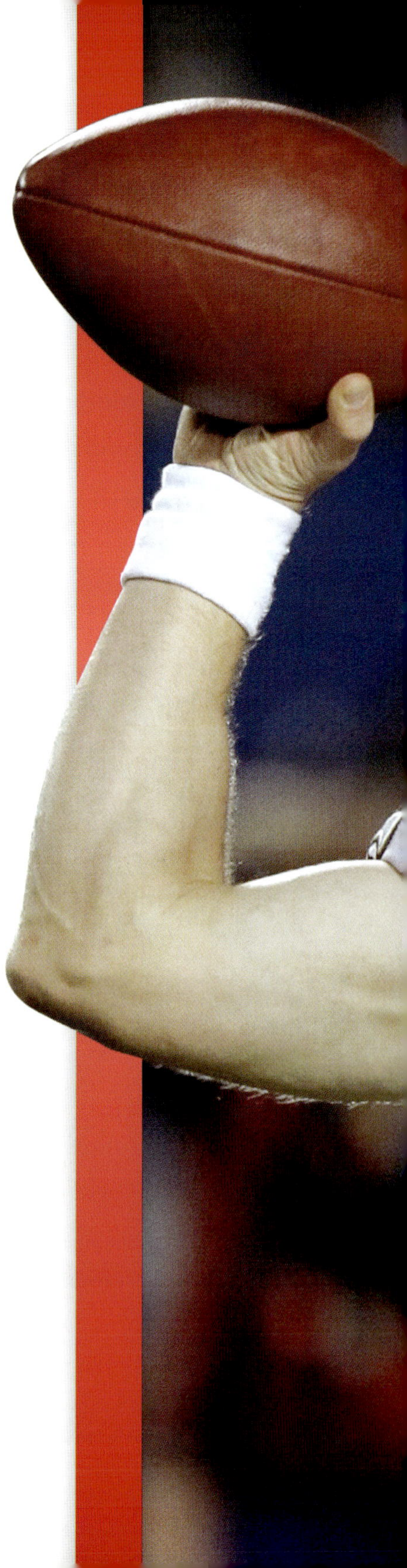

Drew Brees looks to throw in Super Bowl XLIV. He threw two touchdowns in the game.

Emmitt Smith ran thirty times for 132 yards and two touchdowns in Super Bowl XXVIII.

Quarterbacks often win the award. They touch the ball on every offensive play. But other players can have a huge **impact**, too.

Running back Emmitt Smith played in three Super Bowls. His Dallas Cowboys won all three. Smith was at his best in Super Bowl XXVIII. It took place after the 1993 season. Buffalo Bills defenders tried to take him down. But Smith was too powerful. His late touchdown put the game out of reach. It was his second of the day.

RETURN FOR GLORY

Offensive players usually win Super Bowl MVP. Defensive players do sometimes. But special teams players almost never do. Desmond Howard of the Green Bay Packers was the first. He won in Super Bowl XXXI after the 1996 season. Howard returned a kickoff 99 yards for a touchdown.

Wide receivers also make big plays. Time was running out. Santonio Holmes got to the corner of the end zone. He had hardly any space. The Pittsburgh Steelers star leaped high. He grabbed the pass. Then he set both feet down. The play sealed the win in Super Bowl XLIII on February 1, 2009. Holmes was the game's MVP.

Fans shouldn't forget about defensive stars, too. Von Miller made sure the Carolina Panthers couldn't forget about him in February 2016. The Denver Broncos linebacker was everywhere in Super Bowl 50. He had 2.5 sacks and forced two fumbles. He became the tenth defensive player to win Super Bowl MVP.

FUN FACT

Dallas Cowboys teammates Harvey Martin and Randy White shared MVP of Super Bowl XII, the only time there have been co-MVPs.

Santonio Holmes

WHERE SUPER BOWL MVPS LINED UP

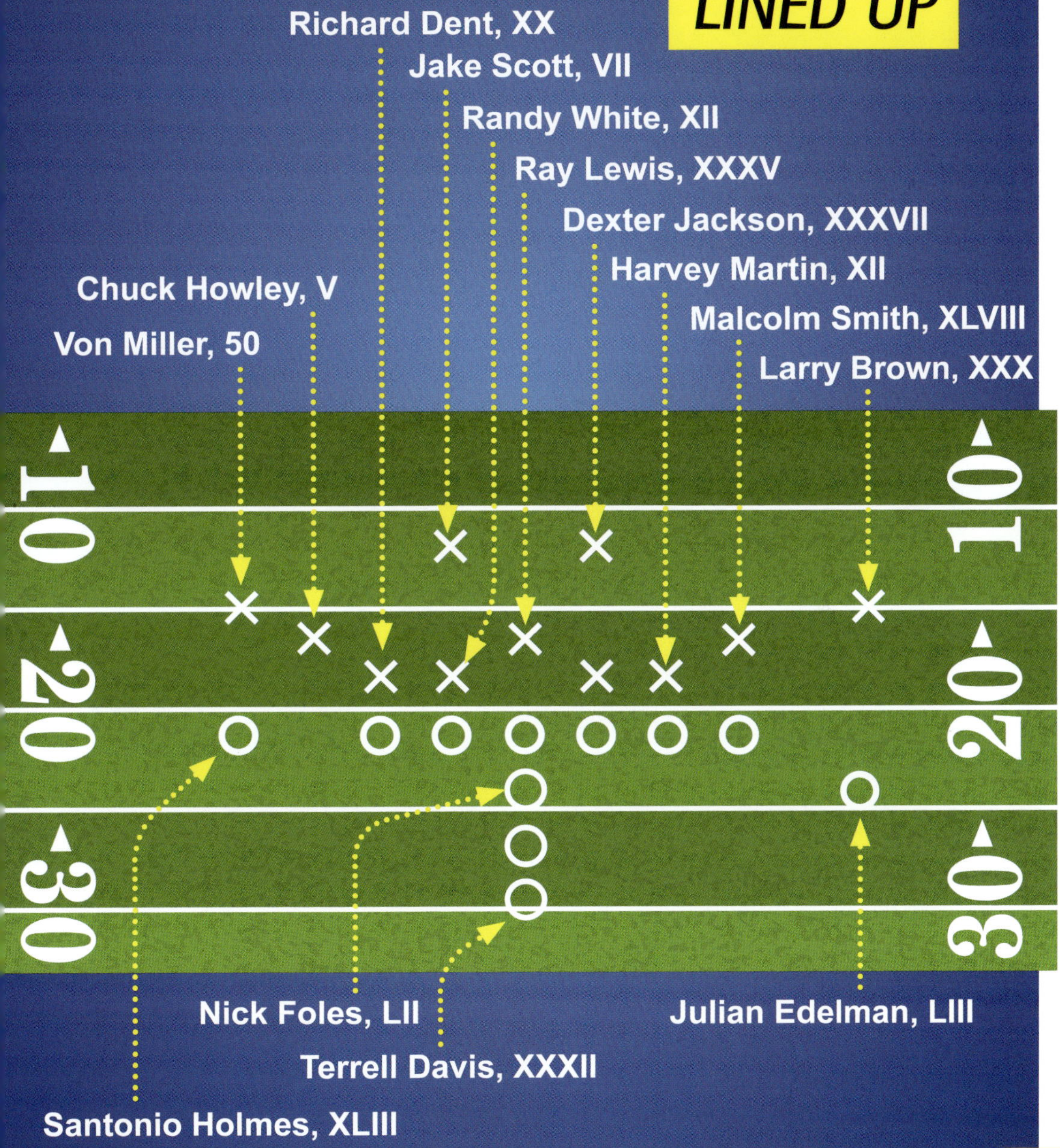

CHAPTER 3

Joe Montana walks off the field after throwing five touchdowns in Super Bowl XXIV.

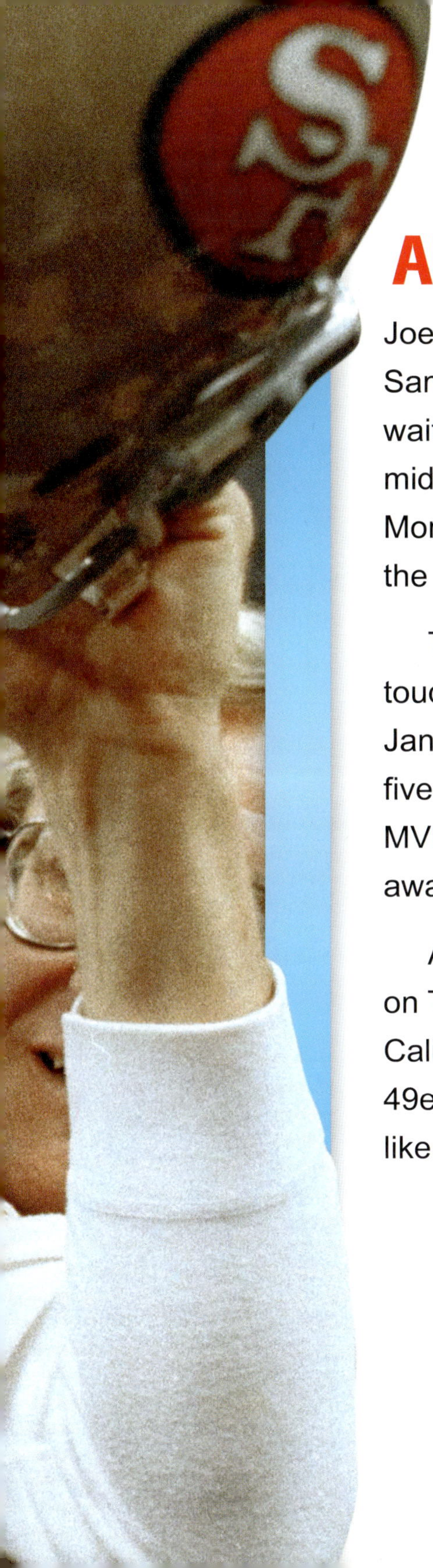

All-Time Greats

Joe Montana goes back to pass. The San Francisco 49ers quarterback waits. His receiver is running up the middle. It's Jerry Rice. And he's open! Montana throws it deep. Rice makes the catch. Touchdown!

They connected for three touchdowns in Super Bowl XXIV in January 1990. Montana threw for five total. He was named Super Bowl MVP. It was his third time winning the award. That set a new record.

A young Tom Brady was watching on TV. He lived nearby in northern California. Brady grew up a big 49ers fan. He wanted to be just like Montana.

FUN FACT

The Dallas Cowboys had seven MVPs as of 2019, the most of any team.

Brady played quarterback, too. He was a star in college. Then the New England Patriots chose him in the NFL Draft. Few expected Brady to have a career like Montana. But he was even better.

Brady is on the field with the Patriots. It is late in Super Bowl LI. It is after the 2016 season. Brady hands the ball off. Running back James White runs outside. He gets in the end zone! Brady hugs his teammates. He has just won his fifth Super Bowl. The Patriots had been behind 28–3. But Brady's calm passing led them back. Afterward, the announcer hands the MVP trophy to Brady. He now has four Super Bowl MVPs. He has beaten Montana's record.

Tom Brady threw the fifteenth Super Bowl touchdown of his career in Super Bowl LI.

FUN FACT

Brady won his first MVP in 2002 in the Patriots' first Super Bowl win.

Only five players have won more than one Super Bowl MVP. These players are the best of the best. And they are all quarterbacks. Bart Starr was MVP of Super Bowl I and II. Terry Bradshaw went back-to-back in XIII and XIV. Montana set a new record with three. Then Brady grabbed it with four.

Brady is the king for now. But Eli Manning of the New York Giants beat him twice. Manning won MVP in Super Bowl XLII and XLVI.

Eli Manning passes in Super Bowl XLVI.

TIMELINE OF SUPER BOWL MVPs

1960

January 15, 1967
Bart Starr wins the first Super Bowl MVP award.

1970

January 17, 1971
Dallas Cowboys linebacker Chuck Howley becomes the first defensive player to win the award, and also the first player on a losing team.

1980

January 20, 1980
Pittsburgh Steelers quarterback Terry Bradshaw becomes the second player to win back-to-back MVP awards.

1990

January 28, 1990
San Francisco 49ers quarterback Joe Montana wins his record third Super Bowl MVP award.

January 26, 1997
The Green Bay Packers' Desmond Howard becomes the first special teams player to win Super Bowl MVP.

2000

February 1, 2004
New England Patriots quarterback Tom Brady becomes the first repeat Super Bowl MVP since Montana.

2010

February 5, 2012
New York Giants quarterback Eli Manning becomes the fifth player to win multiple Super Bowl MVP awards.

February 5, 2017
Brady breaks Montana's record with his fourth Super Bowl MVP award, the most of any player.

2020

February 3, 2019
Patriots wide receiver Julian Edelman wins Super Bowl MVP, becoming one of just two Patriots not named Tom Brady to win.

CHAPTER 4

Big Game Breakouts

Malcolm Smith runs backward. The Seattle Seahawks linebacker watches the play. Denver Broncos quarterback Peyton Manning passes the ball. A receiver waits. But he's too late. Smith steps in and grabs the ball. He starts running to the end zone.

His teammates follow. No one can catch him. Touchdown! The Seahawks defense **dominated** Super Bowl XLVIII on February 2, 2014. Smith was named the game's MVP.

Not all Super Bowl MVPs are big stars. Smith never made a Pro Bowl. Few had heard of him before this play. But few will forget the game he had.

Malcolm Smith runs away from Denver Broncos players to the end zone in Super Bowl XLVIII.

The New England Patriots were dominant. The 2014 and 2016 Patriots had won the Super Bowl. Now the 2017 Patriots were back in the big game. Most fans expected them to beat the Philadelphia Eagles. After all, the Eagles' starting quarterback was hurt.

Backup Nick Foles stands and yells for the ball. The play starts. He sees Zach Ertz run past his defender. Foles zips a pass to the tight end. Ertz brings it in. Then he dives over the goal line. Touchdown! Foles helped Philadelphia to a Super Bowl win. He got the MVP trophy for his performance.

Foles even caught a touchdown pass in the second quarter of the Super Bowl.

NICK FOLES

IN SUPER BOWL LII

LONGEST PASS	55 YARDS
PASSING TOUCHDOWNS	3
PASSER RATING	106.1
RECEIVING TOUCHDOWNS	1
PASSING YARDS	373

Julian Edelman makes a cut to gain yardage in Super Bowl LIII.

The Patriots were back the next year. This time they played the Los Angeles Rams. Quarterback Tom Brady led the way. But one teammate stepped up big. On a third down play, Brady dropped back to pass. Julian Edelman ran up and then to the right. He crossed the field. Brady hit him with a pass. A defender brought Edelman down. But he got the first down.

Soon the Patriots faced another third down. The Rams defense was ready to stop New England. But Brady found Edelman again. A defender soon tackled him. But Edelman again earned a first down. In total, he caught 10 passes for 141 yards. The Patriots won their record sixth Super Bowl. For his efforts, Edelman was named Super Bowl LIII MVP.

It takes a whole team to win a Super Bowl. All players are valuable. But it takes a special one to be Super Bowl MVP.

FUN FACT

Quarterbacks won 29 of the first 54 Super Bowl MVP awards.

BEYOND THE BOOK

After reading the book, it's time to think about what you learned. Try the following exercises to jumpstart your ideas.

THINK

THAT'S NEWS TO ME. Joe Montana won three Super Bowl MVP awards during his career. How might news sources be able to fill in more detail about these games? What new information could you find in news articles? Where could you go to find those sources?

CREATE

PRIMARY SOURCES. A primary source is an original document, photograph, or interview. Make a list of different primary sources you might be able to find about Super Bowl MVPs. What new information might you learn from these sources?

SHARE

SUM IT UP. Write one paragraph summarizing the important points from this book. Make sure it's in your own words. Don't just copy what is in the text. Share the paragraph with a classmate. Does your classmate have any comments about the summary? Do they have additional questions about Super Bowl MVPs?

GROW

REAL-LIFE RESEARCH. What places could you visit to learn more about Super Bowl MVPs? What other things could you learn while you were there?

RESEARCH NINJA

Visit *www.ninjaresearcher.com/0752* to learn how to take your research skills and book report writing to the next level!

RESEARCH

DIGITAL LITERACY TOOLS

SEARCH LIKE A PRO

Learn about how to use search engines to find useful websites.

FACT OR FAKE?

Discover how you can tell a trusted website from an untrustworthy resource.

TEXT DETECTIVE

Explore how to zero in on the information you need most.

SHOW YOUR WORK

Research responsibly—learn how to cite sources.

WRITE

GET TO THE POINT

Learn how to express your main ideas.

PLAN OF ATTACK

Learn prewriting exercises and create an outline.

DOWNLOADABLE REPORT FORMS

Further Resources

BOOKS

Braun, Eric. *Super Bowl Records.* Capstone, 2017.

Doeden, Matt. *The Super Bowl: Chasing Football Immortality.* Millbrook, 2018.

Frisch, Aaron. *Super Bowl Champions: New York Giants.* Creative Education, 2014.

WEBSITES

FACTSURFER

Factsurfer.com gives you a safe, fun way to find more information.

1. Go to www.factsurfer.com.
2. Enter "Super Bowl MVPs" into the search box and click 🔍.
3. Select your book cover to see a list of related websites.

Glossary

dominated: When one team performs much better than the other, they are said to have dominated that team. The 49ers dominated the Broncos in the Super Bowl.

drive: A drive is a single possession for an offense. The Broncos tied the game on a 97-yard touchdown drive.

end zone: The end zone is where someone has to go to score a touchdown. Emmitt Smith burst through into the end zone.

frustrated: Someone is frustrated if they are upset or angry about something. Nick Foles was frustrated when he threw an interception in the Super Bowl.

handoff: In football, a handoff happens when one player gives the ball directly to another. Emmitt Smith got the handoff from the quarterback.

impact: The effect something has on someone or something is called its impact. Julian Edelman's catches in the Super Bowl had a big impact on the Patriots winning the game.

Index

PHOTO CREDITS

The images in this book are reproduced through the courtesy of: Paul Jasienski/AP Images, front cover (left); Paul Spinelli/AP Images, front cover (center), p. 25 (Nick Foles); Seth Wenig/AP Images, front cover (right), p. 3; EFKS/Shutterstock Images, front cover (background); Ed Reinke/AP Images, pp. 5, 6–7; Tom DiPace/AP Images, p. 8; Jeff Bukowski/Shutterstock Images, p. 9; Julie Jacobson/AP Images, pp. 10–11; Susan Ragan/AP Images, p. 12; Red Line Editorial, pp. 13, 21 (timeline), 25 (chart); John Bazemore/AP Images, p. 14; Lennox McLennon/AP Images, pp. 16–17; Eric Gay/AP Images, pp. 18–19; Ben Liebenberg/AP Images, p. 20; Chris O'Meara/AP Images, pp. 22–23; Damian Strohmeyer/AP Images, pp. 24, 26; dean bertoncelj/Shutterstock Images, pp. 27, 30.

ABOUT THE AUTHOR

Kevin Frederickson is a freelance writer and editor from Ohio. He lives near Cincinnati with his golden doodle, Max.